PCCLC

How to Be a
BIGGER
BUNNY

How to Be a BIGGER BUNNY

Written by
FLORENCE MINOR

Illustrated by
WENDELL MINOR

KATHERINE TEGEN BOOKS
An Imprint of HarperCollins Publishers

Tickles the bunny yawned.
It was time to get out of bed.

She called to her bunny family:
"Nibbles! Wiggles!
Giggles! Jiggles!"

But nobody answered.

"Not again!"

Her brothers and sisters had gone on another adventure without her.

"Well," she thought, "I'll just read my new book instead."

How to Be a Bigger Bunny was filled with
adventure stories that Tickles loved to read.

The first story, "Never Give Up,"
was about a little bunny, just like her,
who wanted to climb a very tall tree.
The tree was SO tall,
the little bunny didn't know if
she could ever get to the top.

The story showed how important it is
to keep trying and to never give up.

Tickles fell asleep and
in her dream she climbed a tall tree.

When you never give up,
you can do amazing things!

When Tickles woke up,
her bunny family still wasn't home,
so she read another story.
"How to Be Like a Pirate"
showed her how to act and talk boldly.
So she practiced being like a pirate, too.

"ARRR. AHOY, MATEY!"

While Tickles was reading
"How to Think Your Way out of Tricky Places,"
which had good advice about nibbling,
her bunny family was hopping right into a log on the hillside.

The log was big and hollow.
All of a sudden, she heard: *Crash!*

"Uh-oh," said Tickles. "I wonder what that was."

The sun was setting
and the bunnies had been gone all day.

"Nibbles? Wiggles?" Tickles called.
"Giggles? Jiggles?"

Nobody answered, so Tickles hopped off
to look for them.

"Hello?" Tickles called.
"Helloooo? Is anyone there?"
Nothing.
She called out again.
There was still no answer.
She listened carefully, and guess what?
She heard thumping.

Just then she saw a log on the hillside—
and it was shaking!

In her best pirate talk, Tickles yelled,
"Ahoy there!"

Soon she spotted something pink and
twitching, just like a bunny nose.

It WAS a bunny nose!

Twitch. Twitch.
Thump. Thump.

"Help!" cried her bunny family.
"A rock rolled down the hill
and we're trapped!"

Tickles touched noses with Wiggles.
"Don't worry," said Tickles.
"I'll push that rock away
and save you."

First she pushed the rock.
"Ouch!"

Then she tried again.
"Ooof!"

"I know," she said.
"I'll hop on top of the rock
and it will roll away!"
She climbed a tree, just like in her dream.
"Weeee!" she squealed.

She thought she would land on
the rock, but oops!

Tickles lost her balance.

"Never give up.
Never give up.
NEVER give up,"
she told herself.
Then she remembered the story in her book,
"How to Think Your Way out of Tricky Places,"
and the part about nibbling your way
out of trouble.

So she nibbled and she nibbled and
she nibbled, but it wasn't enough.

After a rest, Tickles nibbled
again as fast as she could.

Chip. Chip. Chip.

Finally, Wiggles's face appeared.
Then came his floppy ears.

Soon Wiggles hopped out, and right behind him
were Giggles, Nibbles, and Jiggles, too.

"Yay for Tickles! You saved us!" they shouted.
"You are the smartest," said Wiggles.
"Bravest," said Giggles.

"Biggest," said Jiggles.
"Best bunny of all!" said Nibbles.
And they all hopped home together.

That night, Tickles dreamed
she was a super bigger bunny,
saving her bunny family
from danger everywhere!

In the morning, her brothers and sisters
found Tickles in her favorite reading place.

"Tickles, you're coming with us today," they said.
"We're never, ever going on an adventure
without you again."

And they never did.

For Katherine Tegen—
editor extraordinaire, and best bunny of them all!
—F.M.

In honor of some of my favorite legends of the past—
Beatrix Potter, Leonard Weisgard, and Garth Williams
—W.M.

Never give up!

Katherine Tegen Books is an imprint of HarperCollins Publishers.

How to Be a Bigger Bunny
Text copyright © 2017 by Florence Minor
Illustrations copyright © 2017 by Wendell Minor
All rights reserved. Manufactured in China.
No part of this book may be used or reproduced in any
manner whatsoever without written permission except in the case
of brief quotations embodied in critical articles and reviews. For
information address HarperCollins Children's Books, a division of
HarperCollins Publishers, 195 Broadway, New York, NY 10007.
www.harpercollinschildrens.com

ISBN 978-0-06-235255-2

The art for this book was created using gouache watercolor on
Strathmore 500 Bristol.
Typography by Rachel Zegar
16 17 18 19 20   SCP   10 9 8 7 6 5 4 3 2 1
❖
First Edition